D1364631

Ellis Island

A Level Three Reader

By Cynthia Klingel and Robert B. Noyed

The Child's World®

On the cover...
This picture shows what Ellis Island and its buildings
look like from high above.

Published by The Child's World®, Inc.
PO Box 326
Chanhassen, MN 55317-0326
800-599-READ
www.childsworld.com

Photo Credits
© A&L Sinibaldi/Tony Stone Images: 17
© Cosmo Condina/Tony Stone Images: 22
© David Forbert/Photri, Inc: 21
© Frank Orel/Tony Stone Images: 26
© Hulton Getty: 6, 9
© Photri, Inc.: 14, 18, 25
© Roger Tully/Tony Stone Images: cover
© 1994 Stephen Graham/Dembinsky Photo Assoc. Inc.: 10, 13
© 1995 Stephen Graham/Dembinsky Photo Assoc. Inc.: 29
© Travis Evans/Unicorn Stock Photos: 5
© XNR Productions, Inc.: 3

Project Coordination: Editorial Directions, Inc.
Photo Research: Alice K. Flanagan

Library of Congress Cataloging-in-Publication Data
Klingel, Cynthia Fitterer.
Ellis Island / by Cynthia Klingel and Robert B. Noyed.
p. cm. — (Wonder books)
"A level three reader" —Cover.
Summary: Briefly describes the history of Ellis Island, what happened there when it
was used as an immigration station, and how it came to be a national park in 1965.
ISBN 1-56766-823-2 (lib. bdg. : alk. paper)
1. Ellis Island Immigration Station (N.Y and N.J.)—Juvenile literature.
[1. Ellis Island Immigration Station (N.Y. and N.J.) 2. United States—Emigration and immigration.
3. National parks and reserves.]
I. Noyed, Robert B.   II. Title.   III. Wonder books (Chanhassen, Minn.)

JV6484 .K56   2000
304.8'73—dc21   99-057778

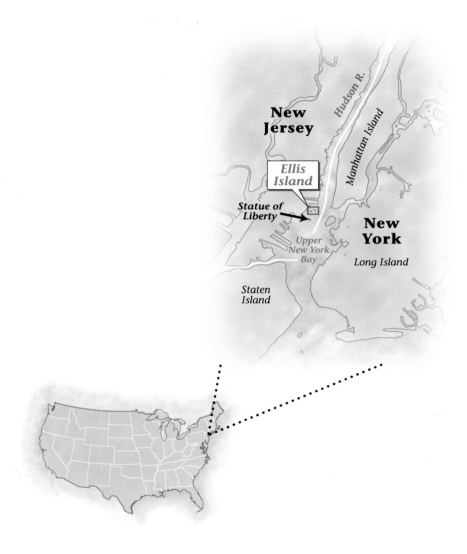

Do you know where Ellis Island is?
Here is a map to help you find it.

The United States is a place where many people come to live. People who move to our country are called **immigrants.** In the early 1900s, Ellis Island was the first stop for many immigrants.

This picture shows a main building of Ellis Island as seen from a boat.

From 1892 to 1954, Ellis Island was used to **process** immigrants. Ellis Island is located on the East Coast of the United States. It is in New York Harbor. It lies within both New York and New Jersey.

Here an immigrant (on the right) is getting his papers checked by workers at Ellis Island.

At that time in history, immigrants traveled to the United States by ship. Many immigrants came from Europe. They stopped at Ellis Island before moving into the United States.

8

This immigrant family has just landed at Ellis Island and is getting ready to leave their boat.

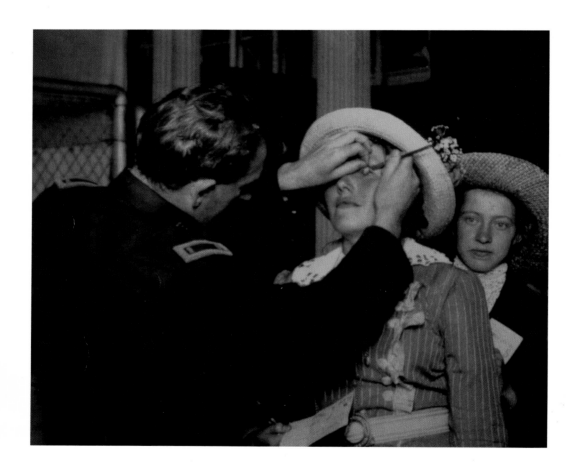

Ships arrived at Ellis Island. Immigrants then got off their ships. They went into buildings and were checked by doctors. Other workers at Ellis Island asked them their names and other things.

The immigrants (on the right) in this picture are getting their eyes checked by an Ellis Island worker.

Many immigrants did not speak English. It was not easy for some immigrants to understand. This was often a hard time for immigrants.

This immigrant family has just arrived at Ellis Island. →

Ellis Island was used until 1954. Between 1892 and 1954, more than 12 million immigrants came through Ellis Island. Four out of ten people alive today had family members come through Ellis Island.

This picture shows a boat full of immigrants as it sails to New York.

The name Ellis Island came from the owner of the island. His name was Samuel Ellis. He sold the island to the state of New York in the early 1800s.

Ellis Island is near the Statue of Liberty in New York Harbor.

17

The state of New York then sold Ellis Island. The United States government paid $10,000 in 1808 for the island. It was then used to process immigrants for more than fifty years.

← These immigrants have just landed at Ellis Island and are gathering their luggage.

In 1965, Ellis Island became a national park. Millions of people raised money to repair the buildings on the island. A museum was also planned for the island. The museum opened in 1990.

This picture shows the main entrance to Ellis Island after it was repaired.

The museum shows the history of Ellis Island. You can see the **historic** Great Hall, where millions of immigrants waited to be **registered.**

← This picture shows the Great Hall of Ellis Island after it was repaired.

You can also see where doctors checked the immigrants. You can see clothing, passports, baggage, and other things. The museum is a very interesting place to visit.

Here are some of the things that were used by doctors on Ellis Island. →

Ellis Island is near another famous **landmark.** The Statue of Liberty can be seen from Ellis Island. The Statue of Liberty is also located in New York Harbor.

This picture shows Liberty Island and the Statue of Liberty.

Ellis Island played an important part in our history. Today, we can visit it and imagine what it was like for immigrants to the United States.

These visitors are looking at a map in the Ellis Island museum.

Glossary

historic (hih-STOR-ik)
When something is historic, it is an important part of the past.

immigrants (IH-mih-grents)
Immigrants are people who come from one country to live in another.

landmark (LAND-mark)
A landmark is a statue, building, or place that is important in history.

process (PRAH-sess)
When immigrants are processed, they are prepared for official entry into another country through a series of steps.

registered (REH-jih-sterd)
When people are registered for something, they are added to an official list.

Index

doctors, 11
Ellis, Samuel, 16
English, 12
Europe, 8
Great Hall, 23
immigrants, 4, 8, 11, 12, 15, 19, 23, 24, 28
museum, 20, 23, 24
national park, 20
New Jersey, 7
New York, 7, 16, 19
New York Harbor, 7, 27
passports, 24
ships, 8, 11
Statue of Liberty, 27
U.S. government, 19

To Find Out More

Books

Jacobs, William Jay. *Ellis Island: New Hope in a New Land.* New York: Simon & Schuster Children's, 1990.

Levine, Ellen, and Wayne Parmenter (illustrator). *If Your Name Was Changed at Ellis Island.* New York: Scholastic, 1994.

Maestro, Betsy C., and Susannah Ryan (illustrator). *Coming to America: The Story of Immigration.* New York: Scholastic, 1996.

Quiri, Patricia Ryon. *Ellis Island.* Danbury, Conn.: Children's Press, 1998.

Temple, Bob. *Ellis Island: Gateway to Freedom.* Chanhassen, Minn.: The Child's World, 2001.

Web Sites

The Ellis Island Home Page
http://www.ellisisland.org/
For information about visiting the island.

The Virtual Ellis Island Tour
http://capital.net/~alta/index.html
For a virtual tour of the island.

Note to Parents and Educators

Welcome to The Wonders of Reading™! These books provide text at three different levels for beginning readers to practice and strengthen their reading skills. Additionally, the use of nonfiction text provides readers the valuable opportunity to *read to learn*, not just to learn to read.

These leveled readers allow children to choose books at their level of reading confidence and performance. Level One books offer beginning readers simple language, word choice, and sentence structure as well as a word list. Level Two books feature slightly more difficult vocabulary, longer sentences, and longer total text. In the back of each Level Two book are an index and a list of books and Web sites for finding out more information. Level Three books continue to extend word choice and length of text. In the back of each Level Three book are a glossary, an index, and a list of books and Web sites for further research.

State and national standards in reading and language arts emphasize using nonfiction at all levels of reading development. The Wonders of Reading™ fill the historical void in nonfiction material for the primary grade readers with the additional benefit of a leveled text.

About the Authors

Cindy Klingel has worked as a high school English teacher and an elementary teacher. She is currently the curriculum director for a Minnesota school district. Writing children's books is another way for her to continue her passion for sharing the written word with children. Cindy Klingel is a frequent visitor to the children's section of bookstores and enjoys spending time with her many friends, family, and two daughters.

Bob Noyed started his career as a newspaper reporter. Since then, he has worked in communications and public relations for more than fourteen years for a Minnesota school district. He enjoys writing books for children and finds that it brings a different feeling of challenge and accomplishment from other writing projects. He is an avid reader who also enjoys music, theater, traveling, and spending time with his wife, son, and daughter.